Snakes
and
Ladders

For the children of Foxfield School

M.M.

To Claire for the support

A.W.

This edition first published in Great Britain 2000
First published in Great Britain 1994
by Egmont Books Ltd,
239 Kensington High St, London W8 6SA
Published in hardback by Heinemann Library,
a division of Reed Educational and Professional Publishing Ltd
by arrangement with Egmont Books Ltd.
Text copyright © Michael Morpurgo 1994
Illustrations copyright © Anne Wilson 2000
The author and illustrator have asserted their moral rights
Paperback ISBN 1 4052 0134 7
Hardback ISBN 0 431 06179 3
10 9 8 7 6 5 4 3 2
A CIP catalogue record for this title is available from the British Library.
Printed and bound in the U.A.E.

Snakes
and
Ladders

Michael Morpurgo

Illustrated by **Anne Wilson**

🍌 **YELLOW BANANAS**

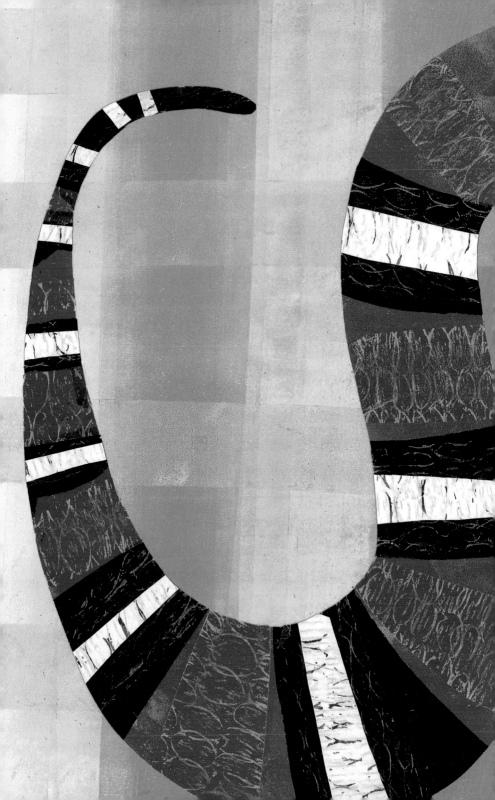

Chapter One

SOME PEOPLE HAVE goldfish or tortoises or hamsters. Wendy's grandad had a snake, a King-snake called Slinky. He was black and gold with little beady eyes and an ever-flicking forked tongue.

Slinky lived in a glass tank on top of the chest-of-drawers in Grandad's bedroom. And that, said Wendy's mother, was exactly where he had to stay.

If Wendy wanted to play with Slinky, then she had to do it in Grandad's bedroom and SHUT THE DOOR.

Wendy was small and thin and quiet.
Hopscotch and handstands were never her idea
of fun. So at school they called her 'weedy
Wendy'. Sad stories made her cry, and so did
Simon McTavish when he kept teasing her about
being poor or about not having a father. So they
called her 'weepy Wendy'. She hated school,
and most of all she hated Simon McTavish.

When she got home from school her mother was out at work like she always was and Grandad was still out in his garden. She sat on the bed in Grandad's room and told Slinky all about Simon McTavish and the horrible things he'd said that day. 'And anyway, we're not poor,' she went on. 'And I have got a dad. He just doesn't live here any more, that's all.'

Slinky flicked out his tongue, which was his way of asking for his tea. He always had a mouse for his tea, a dead one, of course.

When he'd finished swallowing it, Wendy wrapped him round her neck like a scarf and stroked him in between his eyes where he liked it. She hummed him his favourite tune, a jingle from the television, the one about the washing-up liquid that keeps your hands soft.

Grandad came in from the garden. He loved his garden, especially his vegetables. The garden backed on to the park, so he could lean on his fork and watch the football whenever he felt like it. He loved his football almost as much as his garden.

'That cauliflower will be perfect,' he said, wiping his hands on a towel. 'By the time I get back, it'll be just right. We'll have it for Christmas.'

'Why, where are you going?' Wendy asked.

'Hospital,' he patted his side. 'New hip. Nothing to worry about. The old one's worn itself right out.'

Chapter Two

NEXT DAY THEY took Grandad into hospital on the way to school. Wendy's mother was silent with worry. Grandad tried to cheer her up, but it didn't work. He turned to Wendy.

'Now, my girl, you will look after Slinky for me, won't you? No tit-bits, mind. Just his two regular mice, one for his breakfast, one for his tea. And keep an eye on my cauliflower. Any sign of frost, cover it up.'

The car came to a stop.

'I'll see myself in,' he said, and he was gone.

Wendy's mother never said a word all the

way to school. The first person Wendy saw at school was Simon McTavish. He was roaring around the playground whirling his bag above his head. Wendy took a deep breath and walked into school hoping he wouldn't notice her.

'Now then, children,' Mrs Paterson began. 'I've had an idea. And where do I always have my best ideas?'

'In the bath,' they chorused.

'Quite right,' she laughed. 'Well now, I was in my bath last night and I was wondering what we should do for the Parents' Evening this Christmas. Year Three are doing the Nativity play this year. Year Four are cooking the mince pies and Year Five are decorating the hall. What shall we do? I know, I thought, Year Six will put on an exhibition of "Interesting Things" in the front hall, so that people will have

something to look at while they're eating their mince pies. Well, what do you think?'

Simon McTavish pretended to yawn noisily, but she ignored him.

'Well then, why don't we all try to bring in something really interesting, something from the past maybe, something from a far-off country, something amazing, something special.'

Mrs Paterson did go on a bit, but Wendy liked her because she laughed a lot.

'Now, can anyone think of something they'd like to bring in?' Mrs Paterson asked. 'Sarah, what about you?'

Sarah said she had a three-legged milking stool. Sharon had a telescope and Vince said he'd bring in a fox's tail.

'And how about you, Wendy?' she said.

There was only one thing Wendy could think of.

'We've got this old war helmet, Miss,' she said. 'It's my grandad's. He had it in the war. It's a bit rusty though.'

'Like your grandad then,' said Simon McTavish and everyone sniggered. Wendy felt the tears coming.

'A helmet will be just fine, Wendy,' said Mrs Paterson quickly. Then she turned to Simon. 'And Simon McTavish, you've got a brain like a soggy Weetabix.'

Now they were all laughing at Simon instead, and Wendy suddenly felt a lot better. But for the rest of the day she kept finding Simon McTavish looking at her. There was a very nasty smile on his face.

Chapter Three

GRANDAD HAD HIS hip operation the next
day. Wendy's mother rang the hospital that
evening to find out how he was. He was fine
they said, still a bit woozy, but doing well.
They went in to visit him the following
evening. He didn't look very well to Wendy.
He was thin and pale, with one tube in his
arm and another one up his nose. But he
seemed happy enough.

'All done,' he said. 'Good as new. I'll be
playing football inside a week. How's Slinky?
Haven't you brought him in to see me, then?'

And they all laughed at that. Wendy liked to see her mother laugh. She didn't laugh much these days, not since Dad had gone away and left them.

Wendy remembered to ask Grandad about borrowing his helmet from the war.

'Course you can,' he said, 'just so long as you look after old Slinky like I said, and my cauliflower.'

'Promise,' said Wendy.

That evening she told Slinky all about Grandad and his tubes. She fed him his mouse and hummed him his tune and wrapped him around her neck. She stroked him between the eyes, and told him some of the interesting things the other children were bringing in, like Bindi's wooden elephant and Paul's baseball bat.

'But,' she said, 'no one's got a helmet like Grandad's. I'm going to clean it up a bit and then take it into school tomorrow. It'll be the best thing there, you'll see.'

By the time she got to school in the morning, with the helmet in her bag, there was already a huge crowd in the cloakroom. Simon McTavish was there. He stood up on the bench and smiled at her as she came in, only it wasn't a real smile. Then he bent down. When he stood up again there was a helmet on his head, not a battered old rusty war helmet, but a gleaming yellow firefighter's helmet.

'Well, Weedy, what d'you think?' he said. 'My dad collects them. We've got four more at home. But then, some of us haven't got dads, have we?'

She turned away and took off her coat before they could see she was crying.

She told Slinky all about it that evening
when they came back from seeing Grandad
in the hospital.

'That Simon McTavish, he did it on purpose,
I know he did,' she said fiercely. 'I could kill
him, Slinky, I really could. I mean, what would
Grandad's rusty old thing look like next to his?
They'd just laugh at it. I left it in my bag. I never
showed anyone. I told Mrs Paterson I'd changed
my mind. I think she knew, though. She's not
daft. I said I'd bring in something else tomorrow,
but I haven't got anything else, have I?'

As she was speaking, Slinky was looking right into her eyes. He was trying to tell her something.

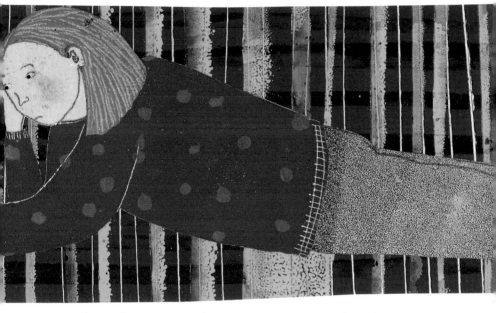

'What about me?' he was saying. 'Why don't you take me?'

Mad, she thought. Ridiculous. Then she thought again. No, it wasn't. It was brilliant. It was the most brilliant idea in the world! She laughed, kissed Slinky on his nose and made up her mind. She would wait until the morning of the Christmas Evening and then take Slinky with her into school.

Chapter Four

BY THE TIME the great day came Wendy had it all worked out. She gave Slinky his breakfast. Then she had her own. She picked up her red lunch-box from the kitchen as usual. Once in Grandad's room, she put her lunch-box in her bag and curled Slinky around it carefully.

'You're not to move,' she whispered, as she closed her bag and buckled it up.

All the way to school she sat in the back of the car and hugged her bag close. Her mother was talking to her over her shoulder.

'Grandad's coming home tonight,' she said, and she wiped the steam off the windscreen. 'I'll bring him along to the Parents' Evening if he's well enough. Did you feed that horrible snake this morning?'

Wendy was thinking it was a good thing that snakes didn't bark or quack or squeak.

'Your dad couldn't stand snakes either, nor spiders come to that. And what do we end up with? Snakes in the bedroom and spiders in the bathroom. No wonder he ran off! Still, we manage, don't we, dear?'

'Course we do, Mum,' said Wendy, and they smiled at each other in the rear-view mirror. They pulled up outside the school gates.

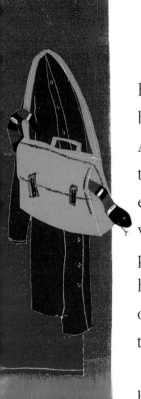

Wendy left her bag hanging up with her anorak in the cloakroom. It would be safe enough till Assembly was over. Assembly was all Christmas carols, and then Mrs Green, the Headteacher, told everyone to have a look at Year Six's wonderful exhibition. The hallowe'en pumpkin was wearing a firefighter's helmet, she said. And there'd be lots of other surprises. More than you know, thought Wendy, more than you know.

Simon McTavish thumbed his nose at her from across the hall.

'You just wait, Simon McTavish,' she said under her breath. 'You just wait.'

As soon as Assembly was over she raced back to the cloakroom. She knew at once that something was wrong. The bag was light, far too light. She looked inside. Slinky was gone, but not all of him. He'd left his skin behind.

Wendy searched everywhere, under the benches, in the toilets, everywhere.

'Wendy, I've been looking for you all over.'

It was Mrs Paterson. As they walked together along the corridor, she said:

'And did you bring something for the exhibition, like you said you would?'

'Yes, Miss,' Wendy said, still looking around her. He couldn't have gone far. He couldn't have.

She was at her table still clutching her bag when Mrs Paterson clapped her hands.

'Now then, children,' she began. 'Wendy has something for us, haven't you, Wendy?'

All heads swivelled. All eyes were on her.

She opened her bag. It was either the red lunch-box or the snakeskin. She picked up Slinky's cast-off skin and held it up between thumb and forefinger. Simon McTavish was laughing like a drain, and so was everyone else, except Mrs Paterson.

'That is wonderful,' she said. 'A snakeskin, a real snakeskin.'

The laughing stopped.

'That's the most wonderful thing we've had. And do you know why? Well, I'll tell you.

Because it's a miracle of nature, a real wonder of the world. Where on earth did you get it from, Wendy?'

She shrugged her shoulders.

'I just found it,' she said, liking Mrs Paterson more than ever. She'd even stopped worrying about Slinky. She'd find him in break. He'd be curled up somewhere asleep. He'd be all right.

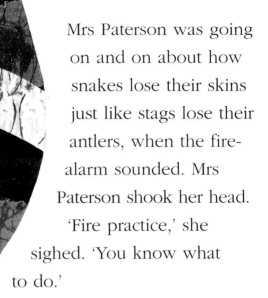

Mrs Paterson was going on and on about how snakes lose their skins just like stags lose their antlers, when the fire-alarm sounded. Mrs Paterson shook her head. 'Fire practice,' she sighed. 'You know what to do.'

They lined up in the corridor and walked out into the playground where they all stood in long cold lines waiting to be counted.

The teachers were gathered in a huddle around Mrs Green who was talking in an animated whisper just loud enough for Wendy to understand most of what she was saying.

' . . . yes, I am quite sure . . . in the cloakroom . . . but it could be anywhere by now . . . could be deadly. Yes, of course I've rung the police . . . Now, I want the children counted carefully and I want all the doors

locked . . . that way no one can get in and
he can't get out . . . '

The teachers ran off in all directions, except
Mrs Paterson who was talking into Mrs Green's
ear. Both of them were looking at Wendy now,
and then they were coming straight towards her.

'Wendy dear,' said Mrs Paterson. 'That snakeskin you brought in this morning. You told me
you found it.'

'Yes, Miss.'

'Well where did you find it, Wendy?'

'Over by the hedge,' said Wendy, thinking as fast as she could. 'Over there.'

But Mrs Green was still worried, very worried.

'Wendy,' she said, 'you didn't actually touch the snake, did you?'

'No, Miss,' she said. Lying, Wendy thought, is quite easy when you have to. 'I never even saw it, Miss. Just the skin. Honest.'

Mrs Green seemed relieved at that.

She spoke now to everyone.

'Children, we are going to have to stay out

here for just a few minutes more. There is nothing whatsoever to worry about, nothing at all. Now why don't we all sing a nice carol to keep ourselves warm?'

They were half-way through 'In the bleak mid-winter', when some of the Infants stopped singing and began to point up at the big chestnut tree by the playground wall. Something was moving high in the branches, something black and gold, and slinky. Someone screamed, and then everyone was shouting and screaming and running. They ran as far from the tree as they could go, as far as the boundary hedge. The teachers rushed over and tried to calm them and comfort them. Only Wendy stayed where she was. Now she had found Slinky, she wasn't going to let him out of her sight. She could hear the police sirens now, but she kept her eye on Slinky all the time.

Chapter Five

TWO POLICE CARS came first, then a fire engine. Flashing and whining, they drove straight through the school gates and into the playground. Police and firefighters leapt out.

Wendy listened hard as Mrs Green explained everything to the police officer, who nodded and then mumbled something Wendy couldn't hear into his radio. He was looking up at Slinky, shielding his eyes against the sun.

'I don't like the look of him,' he said. 'Black and gold. Could be poisonous. I'm not taking any chances, Mrs Green, not with my officers, not with your children. You'd best take the children back inside the school where they can't see. He may have to be shot.'

'No!' Wendy cried. 'No!'

And before anyone could stop her she was up on the playground wall and running along it towards the tree.

She grabbed an overhanging branch, swung herself up and began to climb.

They were shouting up at her to come down,
but she kept climbing.

The higher she climbed the more branches
there were, and the easier it was – until she
looked down. Everyone was so small. The fire
engine was a toy.

Then she saw a policeman with a rifle. He
was aiming at the top of the tree.

'Don't shoot!' she screamed. 'Don't shoot!'
And she climbed again.

When at last she reached Slinky, he was
curled around the highest branch and would
not let go.

'I won't let them hurt you,' she said, stroking
him between the eyes. 'Honest I won't.'

And she hummed him his favourite tune

as she prised him off the branch and wrapped him round her neck. Then the wind blew and the tree swayed and she felt suddenly sick with fear. She clung to the branch and tried not to look down. But she did look. There was a ladder up against the tree, and a firefighter was climbing up towards her.

'Don't move,' he called to her. 'I'm coming. I'm coming.' His face was paper-white under his yellow helmet.

He went on talking as he climbed off the ladder and into the tree.

'What's your name, then?'

'Wendy.'

'Nice name.' He was getting closer all the time. 'I'm Peter, Peter McTavish. My boy Simon, he's in your school. You know him?'

'Yes,' said Wendy. 'I know him.'

'Little horror, isn't he?' he went on, his voice very calm and chatty. 'Still, hardly surprising when you think about it, I suppose. A boy needs his mum, doesn't he?'

'Hasn't he got one, then?' Wendy asked.

'She ran off,' he said.

'I've got a dad that ran off,' Wendy said, stroking Slinky's head between his eyes. The firefighter was on the same branch by now and inching his way towards her. Slinky tickled her ear with his tongue. 'He's hungry,' she said. 'I think he wants his mouse.'

The firefighter looked puzzled.

'You know that snake, don't you?' he said.

'Course I do,' said Wendy. 'He's called Slinky. He belongs to my grandad.'

'So, he's not poisonous, then?'

'No.'

'And he's not strangling you, then?'

'No,' said Wendy. 'You can stroke him if you like.'

'No, thank you.' The firefighter smiled. 'I think I'll just get you down. Can you manage the ladder?'

Wendy shook her head. 'My legs, they've gone all wobbly and I feel sick.'

'Over my shoulder, then,' he said. 'I'll give you a fireman's lift.'

All the way down Wendy kept her eyes closed. 'You sure this snake of yours is friendly?' the firefighter asked. 'He's giving me funny looks.'

'Quite sure,' said Wendy, and she squeezed her eyes even tighter shut.

Then her feet were on the ground and there were other arms around her and she could open her eyes. Everyone was cheering. Mrs Green was crying and Mrs Paterson was crying. They were all crying and laughing at the same time, and Wendy's wobbly legs began to feel better again.

Chapter Six

GRANDAD WAS WELL enough to come along
in a wheelchair for the Christmas Evening. He
wasn't at all cross about Slinky. Wendy told him
everything and he just laughed and laughed.
Wendy's mother pushed him around the school,
smiling proudly whenever anyone talked about
Wendy and how brave she'd been.

Slinky was the star of the show. Curled up in
his tank with his cast-off skin beside him, he
flicked his tongue at everyone and looked very
pleased with himself.

After a bit Wendy wandered off on her own.
She liked being liked. She liked being noticed.
Fame had been fun, but she'd had enough of
it already. She sat down in a corner of the hall
and ate her mince pie.

'Wendy?'

Wendy looked up. It was Simon McTavish.

'I've got something,' he said. It was a
Christmas present.

'For me?' He nodded.

She took it and unwrapped it. It was a game
of Snakes and Ladders.

'That's from my dad,' he mumbled. 'This is from me.'

He handed her a Christmas card. She opened it up. It said:

'Sorry for what I did. Happy Christmas. Love from Simon McTavish.'

When she looked up again, he had gone.

Grandad was up and about by Christmas. They had his cauliflower with their chicken for Christmas dinner, and played Snakes and Ladders all evening with Slinky wrapped around Wendy's neck. It was far and away the best Christmas she'd ever had.

YELLOW BANANAS

Yellow Bananas are brilliantly imaginative stories written by some of today's top writers. These beautifully illustrated books provide an excellent introduction to chapter books.

So if you've enjoyed this story, why not pick another from the bunch?

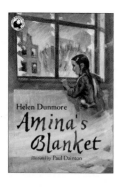

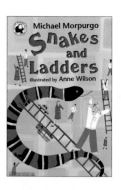